Noel the Coward

by Robert Kraus
pictures by Jose Aruego & Ariane Dewey

Windmill Books and E.P. Dutton | New York

Copyright © Windmill Books
Text copyright © Robert Kraus
Illustrations copyright © Jose Aruego and Ariane Dewey

All Rights Reserved

Published by Windmill Books & E.P. Dutton
201 Park Avenue South, New York, New York 10003

Library of Congress Cataloging in Publication Data

Kraus, Robert,
Noel the coward.

SUMMARY: Coward powered Noel changes to a hero with
the help of Charlie's School of Self Defense.
[1. Courage—Fiction] I. Aruego, Jose. II. Dewey,
Ariane. III. Title.
PZ7.K868No [E] 77-2651

ISBN: 0-525-61565-2

Published simultaneously in Canada by Clarke, Irwin & Company Limited
Toronto and Vancouver

Edited by Robert Kraus
Printed in U.S.A.
10 9 8 7 6 5 4 3 2 1
First Edition

For Charles C. Nelson
Former Instructor
U.S. Marines

Noel was a coward.

So was his father.

"Better a live coward than a dead hero," said Noel's mother.

But Noel wasn't happy being a live coward.

Gus and Tony
punched and teased him.
"Noel, Noel,
Is a coward!

Noel, Noel's
Coward powered,"
they shouted,
throwing sticks and stones.

Noel ran away crying.
"I'm not a coward!
I just don't know
how to fight back!"

"Neither do I,"
said Noel's father.

So they both went to
Charlie's School of Self-Defense.

Charlie was little but tough.
"The bigger they are, the harder I fall,"
he said, shadowboxing. "I mean, the harder
they fall!" he corrected himself.
"Notice my fancy footwork!"

"Can you teach us?" asked Noel.
"You bet," said Charlie.

Noel and his father learned

boxing,

wrestling,   judo,

karate,

kung fu,

and dirty fighting!
"It often comes in handy," said Charlie.

They graduated with honors!

The next day Gus and Tony
punched and teased Noel.

Noel dodged their punches
and ignored their teasing.

He snapped his fingers, gave them
a dirty look and walked away.

He didn't have to fight them
because he *knew* he could!

Gus and Tony knew he could, too,
and they never punched and teased Noel again.
Or Noel's father.

"My heroes!" said Noel's mother.

And they really were.